dan ungureanu

Nara and the Island

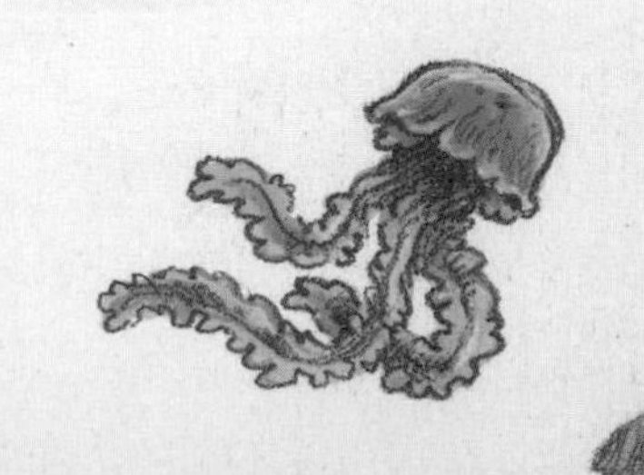

Andersen Press

My home is so small, you can't lose anything.
At least, that's what my dad says.

But sometimes I felt like getting lost

so I would go to my secret hiding place

and look out at the other island.

Then I'd dream about how I'd get over to it.

I could make long legs and run across...

I could ask the birds to fly me there...

I could borrow Dad's bottle collection and empty the sea.

But I would have needed
a million, billion bottles.

So instead of dreaming, I always ended up feeling sad.

Or I did until today, when Dad
found my hiding place.

He says now he's fixed our boat, we can have a real adventure.

He's going to find
the Big Fish.

It's in lots of his books, but no one has ever caught it.

And if I stay close to shore,
I can explore the island
while he rows around it.

Up close, the island is bigger…

and greener and noisier and stranger.

Full of curious shapes, funny sounds and odd-looking things.

It's scary and I want to go home.
But then I meet the biggest surprise of all,
called Aran.

Aran says some of the funny-looking things are his best friends.

I tell him about my home, a little small and quiet, where it's hard to find a hideaway.

He tells me about his home, so noisy and wild,
he's always trying to find a bit that's just his.

Aran has one secret place though. It's so beautiful, he's never shown it to anyone.

But maybe we could share it.

I think I'd like that.

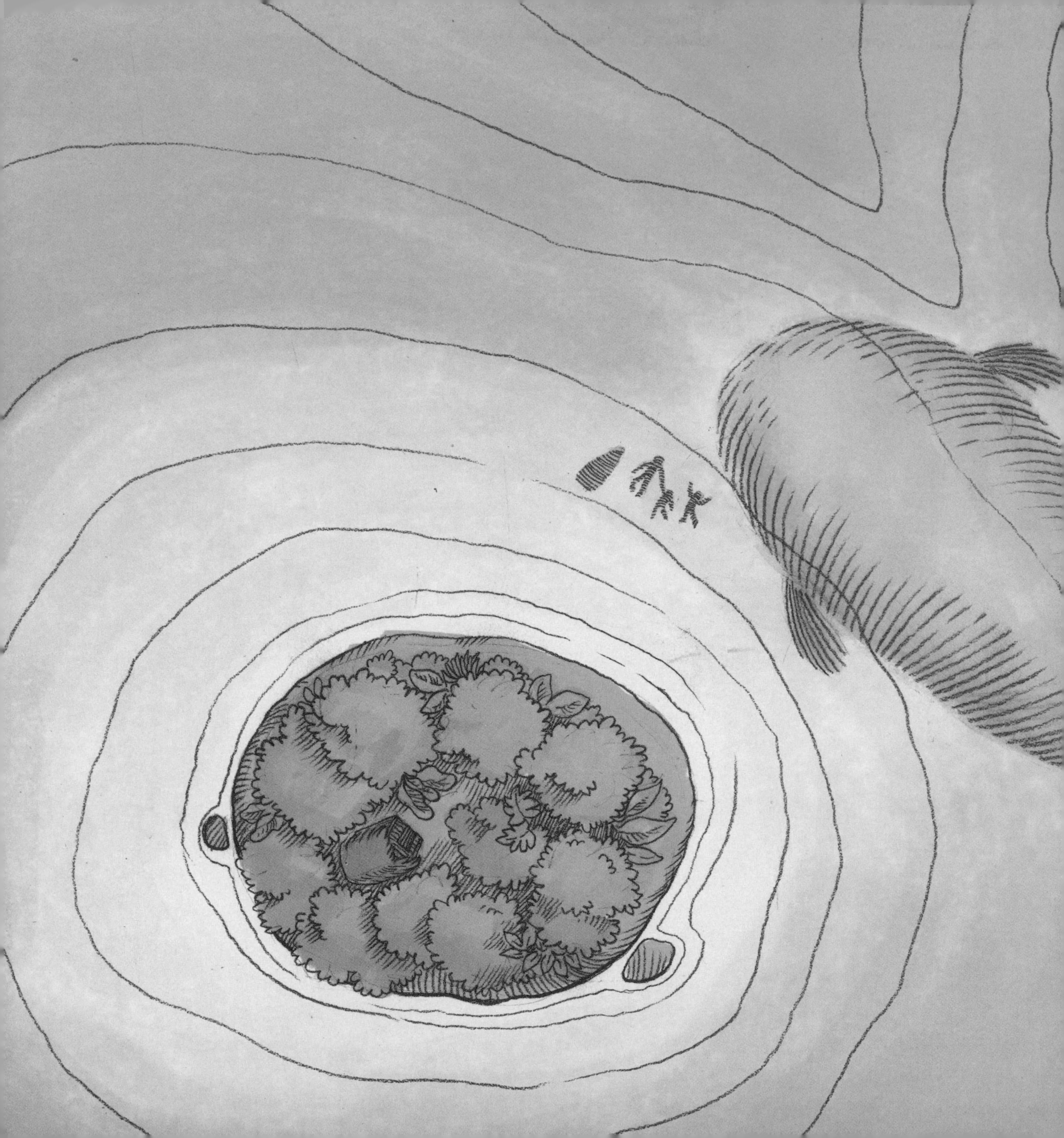